The WISH LIBRARY

Snow Day in May

WISH LIBRARY

Snow Day in May

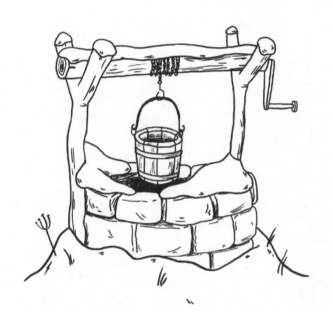

Christine Evans

illustrated by Patrick Corrigan

ALBERT WHITMAN & COMPANY
CHICAGO, ILLINOIS

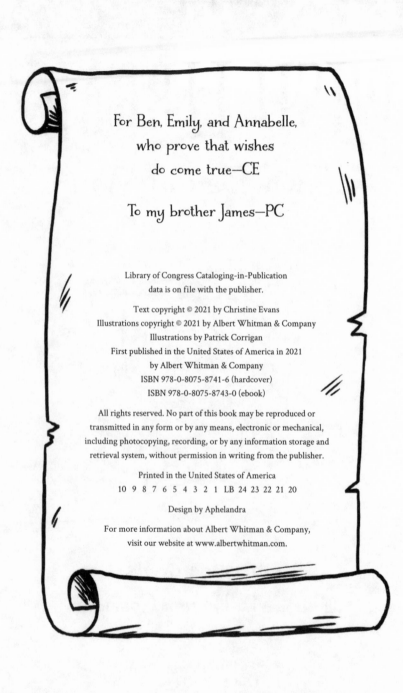

For Ben, Emily, and Annabelle,
who prove that wishes
do come true—CE

To my brother James—PC

Library of Congress Cataloging-in-Publication
data is on file with the publisher.

Text copyright © 2021 by Christine Evans
Illustrations copyright © 2021 by Albert Whitman & Company
Illustrations by Patrick Corrigan
First published in the United States of America in 2021
by Albert Whitman & Company
ISBN 978-0-8075-8741-6 (hardcover)
ISBN 978-0-8075-8743-0 (ebook)

Printed in the United States of America
10 9 8 7 6 5 4 3 2 1 LB 24 23 22 21 20

Design by Aphelandra

For more information about Albert Whitman & Company,
visit our website at www.albertwhitman.com.

Contents

CHAPTER 1

Lucky Pennies

"One, two, three, eyes on me!" Ms. Earl sang from the front of the class.

"One, two, eyes on you," Room 23 chanted back.

Most days, Raven Rose liked her teacher being so cheerful. But today, she did not feel like joining in. Today, Raven wished Ms. Earl would be boring like most grown-ups.

"Before you head out for recess, remember tomorrow is Voices from History day," Ms. Earl said, clapping her hands. "I can't wait to hear all about the people you chose. Don't forget your costumes!"

Raven's hands twisted in her lap. Normally, she loved doing projects. But that was when her best friend, Belle Cunningham, was her partner. They'd spent weeks working on their Voices from History project. Belle had practiced being their historical person: Nellie Bly. Raven had painted the portrait and sewed the costumes with Dad. But now Belle was gone, and Raven was going to have to present on her own. She would have to do a lot of things on her own now.

On the playground, Raven hung upside down on the monkey bars, her glasses dangling. A tiny ladybug buzzed around and landed on her hand.

Belle always said if a ladybug landed on you, you should make a wish. But Raven didn't believe in that stuff. Especially not now.

Only a week ago, they had been hanging on the bars together when Belle had told Raven the news.

"My dad got a new job," Belle had said. "We're moving on Saturday."

"You can't!" Raven had told her. "We're best friends forever!"

"I'm sorry." Belle had dropped to the ground and run off crying.

The thought of school without Belle was terrifying. She had always been the confident one. Being the center of attention made Raven's stomach flip, and not in a fun way like on the monkey bars. Raven's dad called them a perfect pair, like peanut butter and jelly or hot cocoa and marshmallows.

A shadow fell across Raven. The ladybug flew away. "What are you doing?" a voice asked.

It was the new kid, Luca Flores. He'd taken Belle's place in class.

"Just hanging out," said Raven.

"Can I join you?" asked Luca.

"Um. I'm actually finished," said Raven, pulling herself up. She didn't want to hang from the bars with Luca. Even if it wasn't the same now, it had been her and Belle's thing to do together.

Belle was the kind of friend who finished your sentences. Like, if Raven said, "I really want..." Belle would finish, "frozen yogurt!" And she was almost always right. Belle was the kind of friend who made you feel brave. She made faces to make Raven laugh when she was nervous. Or held her hand if she was upset.

Raven ran to the bathroom to wipe away tears before Luca saw.

Back in Room 23, Raven didn't even look up as Luca took the seat next to her. "Are you o—" Luca started to say, but Ms. Earl was speaking.

"I have a fun science experiment to share this afternoon!" the teacher said.

At least in science, Raven didn't have to present anything. She liked experiments—working out what would happen and learning new facts.

Ms. Earl handed out stacks of dull pennies and bottles of vinegar, cola, lemon juice, and water. According to the board, they were going to test which liquid cleaned pennies the best.

"Fill in your worksheets with what you think will happen," Ms. Earl told the class, tapping the board using her wooden pointer with an owl on the end. "Then put a penny in each jar. Add lemon juice to one, vinegar to another, cola to another, and water in the last one, as your control."

Raven filled out her worksheet while Luca examined the materials. "I might keep one of these pennies," he said.

"Why?" asked Raven. "You can't buy anything with a penny."

"No," said Luca. "But I could throw it in a well and make a wish. And wishes can be worth a lot."

Raven just shook her head. If wishes were real, Belle would've been able to stay.

Still, as Raven worked, she thought about what Luca had said. And as she dropped a dull penny into each of the jars, she found herself hoping that, just once, something magical could happen.

CHAPTER 2

Dandelion Wishes

After school, Raven met her younger sister, Izzy, in the schoolyard. Izzy was six and in Ms. Olden's kindergarten class. Raven and Izzy usually kicked a ball around, while Dad chatted with the other parents.

Raven always had a soccer ball with her. Soccer was her favorite sport, and she and Belle played all the time. Raven pulled out the ball from her bag, but she didn't feel much like playing.

"What's wrong?" asked Izzy. "You're being weird."

"I need a way to skip school tomorrow," Raven said quietly.

"Why do you need to skip school?" shouted Izzy.

"Shhh!" hissed Raven. The last thing she needed was for their dad to hear. Raven kicked the ball to Izzy to distract her. "I need to skip so I don't have to present my Voices of History project."

"Huh?" said Izzy. "You love history. You're always watching *boring* history shows."

"They're not boring!" said Raven. "And it's not the history I'm worried about. It's speaking in front of the class. That was supposed to be Belle's job."

"Well, you'd still have to do it the next day, right?" Izzy asked.

"I don't think so. Tomorrow is Voices of History day. If I miss it, I won't have to do it at all," Raven reasoned.

"I don't get it. I love talking to people!" said Izzy.

"You should come do it then!" said Raven, kicking the ball at Izzy harder than she meant to.

"Hey!" said Izzy, rubbing her leg. "There's no way Mom and Dad will let you skip school. Remember the time you pretended you had a rash?"

When they were in first grade, Belle and Raven had covered their faces with red marker dots to avoid a math test. When Raven's dad had stopped laughing, he'd called Belle's mom. They'd both ended up with extra chores. Izzy was right.

Their parents would see through any excuse she thought up.

"I have an idea," said Izzy.

"What is it?"

"Make a wish for school to be closed tomorrow."

Raven stopped the ball with her foot and looked at her little sister. Wishes again. Why did they keep coming up? Raven hadn't told Izzy what Luca had said, had she? Raven shook her head. It must be a coincidence.

"Wishes aren't real, Iz."

"Sure they are. Mom said she threw a penny in a fountain in Rome and wished to go back someday. And she did."

"That's because she's a pilot. She flies all over the world."

"See! It worked. You should try it." Izzy picked a dandelion and held it out. "Blow!"

Raven shook her head. She needed a real way to get out of school tomorrow. "Come on," she said. "Let's practice shooting. I'll be in goal first."

Izzy kicked the soccer ball straight at Raven, as always. Izzy had always preferred gymnastics to soccer.

"You need to curl it!" Raven called. "Kick the side of the ball."

Izzy nodded. She wound up and kicked. But instead of curling, the ball whizzed sideways into the trees. Izzy shrugged and tipped herself into a handstand.

"I'll get it then!" Raven chased after the ball toward the dark trees at the edge of the schoolyard. She ran between two huge chestnut trees, hunting for the ball. At last, she found it underneath a fallen branch. *How had Izzy managed to kick it so far?*

As Raven bent to grab the ball, something glittered in the sunlight. She picked up the shiny object and rubbed away the dirt.

A coin? Where on earth did that come from? Raven

wondered. One side had a smiling woman Raven didn't recognize. The other had some strange writing. Raven slipped the coin into her pocket to show Izzy. But as she turned around to walk back, she tripped.

"Ow!" Raven clutched her ankle and looked for what had tripped her. At her feet was a large pile of stones, arranged in a circle. In the center was a

wooden bucket on a chain, and a handle to bring it up and down.

It was an old well. Raven was sure it hadn't been there before. But a well couldn't appear out of nowhere. That was impossible. And Raven absolutely, positively did not believe in impossible things.

"Raven! Where are you?" Izzy shouted.

"I'll be there in a minute!"

Raven took the gold coin out of her pocket and turned it around and around between her fingers. She remembered what Luca had said about wishes. And then Izzy. Now, Raven had a coin and a well right in front of her.

Raven shook her head; wishes were impossible. She should go back to Izzy.

But...it wouldn't do any harm to try, would it? If she tossed the coin and nothing happened, she'd laugh at herself and move on.

So Raven whispered, "I wish school were canceled tomorrow," and tossed the strange coin into the well.

CHAPTER 3

The Wish Library

Raven tumbled through darkness, trying to grab something to break her fall. But the walls of the well were smooth. She was so terrified, she couldn't even scream. Would she ever stop falling?

At last, Raven landed. But only for a moment. As soon as she reached the bottom, she bounced straight back into the air! Landed. Bounced. And landed again. Finally, she came to rest.

She tried moving. Legs? Check. Arms? Check. Raven rubbed her eyes and patted around until she found her glasses. Raven put them on, relieved they weren't broken.

She had landed on some sort of trampoline. Around her was a massive chamber filled with golden light. Surrounding her were tall shelves stacked with dusty bottles, flasks, test tubes, books, and boxes.

"Where am I?" Raven said. She had been in the forest, throwing a coin in a strange well a few seconds ago. How had she ended up here?

"You're in the Wish Library," a deep voice boomed. Raven jumped and turned around. A tall woman gazed down at her. She was wearing a long, shimmering gown in all the colors of the rainbow. A velvet cloak floated out behind her. She stroked a green bearded dragon perched on her shoulder.

"Who are you?" Raven whispered. Her heart hammered. There had to be an explanation. It was impossible. She must have fallen over in the forest and bumped her head. This was all a dream. It was the only explanation. Izzy would find her in a minute and wake her up.

The woman took out a golden trumpet and held it to her ear. "Say again! I'm a trifle hard of hearing."

"Who are you?" Raven repeated a little louder.

"The Librarian, of course," she shouted, peering over her gold half-moon glasses. "And this is Sebastian," she pointed at the reptile, who was also wearing glasses. "More to the point, who are you?"

"Raven Rose."

"And what brings you to the Wish Library, Raven Rose?" the Librarian bellowed.

"I...I don't know. I was playing soccer, I threw a coin in a well, and then I was here...in this dream."

"Ah, you found the wishing well entrance. It only calls to those who truly need a wish to come true. And for your information, young lady, this is not a dream."

Raven gazed at the never-ending shelves with their strange contents. "So, all these…things…are wishes?" she asked.

"Yes indeed! We have your basic superpowers over here: flying, invisibility, superstrength." The

Librarian waved at a shelf of bubbling test tubes. "Down there, we have baby sisters, puppies, and dragons." This shelf contained bottles and jars filled with shimmering rainbow gases. "And this one is banishments and curses." Here, padlocked chests vibrated and hummed as if they were alive. "You don't want to touch any of those," the Librarian

added, shuddering as if a slug had crawled along her spine.

The Librarian turned to some kind of machine and clattered at a keyboard. The machine looked like a computer, but it was impossibly old. The Librarian stopped typing and turned a giant wheel on the side of the machine. It squeaked like a playground swing, and green numbers and letters appeared on a dusty screen. They moved far too fast for Raven to make sense of them.

"According to my wish computer, you would like school to be canceled, correct?" the Librarian asked.

"Um. I guess so?" Raven said. How could she know that? This was *definitely* a dream.

"Well, do you, or don't you?" The Librarian tapped her foot. "I don't have all day, you know. I have returns to restack, customers to serve, reptiles to walk." Sebastian jumped up and down when he heard her say, "Walk."

"Okay, yes. Yes, please." This was the strangest dream Raven had ever had.

The Librarian pressed more keys and turned the wheel again. Next she pulled a rusty lever, and a printer whirred and spat out a tiny piece of paper.

"Shelf 22-A, Row 199," said the Librarian, gliding down a row lined with shelves of bubbling cauldrons. "This way to the school-related wishes— one of our most popular sections!"

Raven followed. But she couldn't keep up with the Librarian, who was wearing roller skates under her rainbow gown. The Librarian whizzed around a wobbling stack of books.

Raven ran to catch up, but the Librarian had

vanished. Raven stopped to catch her breath. None of this seemed right. She had to find a way to wake up from this dream.

But when Raven slid to the ground and rested her head on her knees, she knew she was not dreaming at all. Tears streamed down her face and plopped onto the dusty floor. Real tears.

Real librarian. Real lizard. Real library.

Raven's tears fell faster.

CHAPTER 4

Read the Small Print

"Now, now, no need to cry!" said the Librarian a few moments later. "You're making a puddle on my floor."

Raven looked up. Sebastian the bearded dragon clutched a test tube filled with sparkling white liquid. He climbed down and held it out to Raven. Tiny gold particles whizzed around inside. Raven grabbed at the test tube, but it slipped through her sweaty fingers. Quickly, the Librarian stuck out her roller skate and saved the tube from breaking on the floor.

"Careful!" she said. "Smashing a wish would be catastrophic!"

Raven could feel tears gathering in the corners of her eyes again, but she blinked them away. She had to figure out what was going on.

"Pick yourself up now. You have paperwork to sign."

Raven followed the Librarian back to the

computer, where a long piece of parchment waited on the printer.

"Here's the contract. Read the small print, please. People never read the small print." The Librarian presented the parchment rolled up like a scroll. "The most important thing to remember is don't be late returning the wish. Fines begin the second you go past the due date. And they can be...unpleasant. *Extremely* unpleasant."

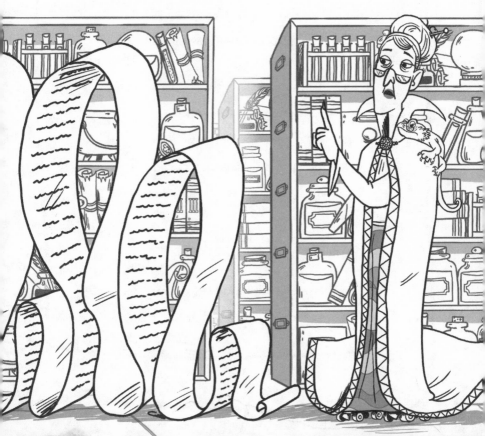

Raven didn't like how the Librarian emphasized "extremely." Raven unrolled the gigantic scroll. It was longer than she was tall, and full of fancy, curly writing.

WISH LIBRARY
EST. 1781

This contract must be signed by the person or animal borrowing a wish from the Wish Library. It is legally and morally binding.

Do not tell anyone about the Wish Library.
Do not reveal the entrance.
Do not tell non-cardholders about your wish.
If you do, you will face the consequences listed below in the small print.

LATE FEES

For each minute past the return time, one consequence will be added to your account.
This contract is binding for life.

Next was even tinier print that Raven assumed were the consequences, but even with her glasses on, she couldn't read them. At the end of the scroll was a space for Raven's name and signature. The Librarian presented a white feather quill. "The wish is due by 11:11 a.m. on Friday."

Signing the contract was a terrible idea. What were the unpleasant consequences? But Raven didn't dare ask the busy Librarian to read them. *I shouldn't sign,* she thought. *I'll go home and forget this ever happened.*

Then Raven's thoughts turned to the next day. She would have to go to school and stand in front of everyone. She would stumble over her words, turn red, and cry. Everyone would laugh and call her a crybaby. They'd probably call her a crybaby for the rest of the year. Maybe even for the rest of school. No consequence could be worse than that. This wish might be her only chance of surviving second grade.

Raven took a deep breath. She scribbled her

signature with the quill and handed the scroll back.

"Excellent! Here's your library card. Keep it safe!" The Librarian handed over a library card which read:

WISH LIBRARY, established 1781

I accept responsibility for all use made on this card

Raven Rose

On the side was Raven's photo. She looked red and blotchy. When had the Librarian taken the photo?

"And here's your wish." The Librarian squatted, which was tricky on roller skates, to look deep into Raven's eyes.

"Don't use the wish until you're ready for it to

take effect," the Librarian said, looking stern. She stood up straight. "And remember, don't be even a second late in returning it."

"Okay," Raven squeaked. She placed the wish in her pants pocket. It was warm, and vibrated as she held it through the fabric. Raven hoped she wouldn't drop it again.

"The instructions are on the side of the test tube. See you back here on Friday."

"Um. How do I get home?" Raven asked.

"Through that door, dear." The Librarian pointed at a door with a flashing neon exit sign. It definitely hadn't been there before. Raven pushed it open. She covered her eyes as a bright light flooded the doorway.

The next thing Raven knew, she was lying on the ground, faceup, with her hands over her eyes.

"Have you been taking a nap back here?" said Izzy.

Raven sat up and looked around. The well had vanished. Had she imagined the whole thing?

"I...umm...fell over," she said.

Izzy pulled her up. "You *are* being weird today. Come on. Dad is waiting." Izzy turned back to the schoolyard.

Raven brushed herself off, trying to make sense of what had just happened. Then she felt something buzzing in her pocket.

The test tube.

There was no doubt about it. The Wish Library was real.

CHAPTER 5

Make a Wish

"You're quiet, Raven. And you've hardly eaten any-thing!" Dad looked worried. "I hope you're not coming down with something."

"I'm fine, just not very hungry," she replied, pushing her favorite, spaghetti and meatballs, around the plate.

"I'll have it!" said Izzy, scooping Raven's left-overs onto her own plate.

Dad stared at Raven. He had asked her something.

"Huh?" Raven said.

"Are you ready for your presentation? Do you want to practice it?"

Raven thought for a second. Maybe the presentation wouldn't be as bad as she feared. Maybe she wouldn't need the wish with the terrible, scary consequences after all. She could return the test tube to the Wish Library and never go near the place again. "Yes, please," said Raven.

"Great! Let's work on it after we've cleaned up from dinner." Dad reached over to Raven's face and picked something off her cheek.

"An eyelash. Make a wish," he said.

"What?" Raven felt dizzy.

"It's a thing," he said with a smile. "You can make a wish on a fallen eyelash."

"No...thank you," Raven stammered. Her stomach churned. Thinking about wishes made her queasy. She touched the test tube in her pocket. It was decided. In the morning, she'd take it straight back to the Wish Library and try to forget all about it.

After working together to load the dishwasher, wipe the table, and pack away the leftovers, Raven and Dad went to the living room to practice. Dad sat on the couch. Raven stood in front of him with her presentation.

"I want to watch too," said Izzy, plonking down next to Dad.

"Okay," said Dad. "But no interrupting."

Raven looked at the floor, took a breath, and began her presentation. Dad smiled and nodded along. But halfway through, Raven stopped. *What came next?*

"And then...I...errr..." Raven felt her cheeks ignite. "I can't remember what I was going to say."

"No problem! This is what rehearsals are for. Read your notes, and try again," said Dad.

Raven shook her head. If she messed up in front of her family, she was sure to do the same at school. "I'll just go to my room," she said. "I'll read the notes in bed, so I'll be ready for tomorrow. Night."

But once in bed, Raven couldn't sleep. She knew she'd stumble over the words in her presentation. Her worst fears would come true.

Raven patted under the pillow to find the test tube she'd hidden there. It hummed like a bee. She climbed down from the top bunk and opened the bedroom door. The door creaked as usual. Raven waited a few seconds, but Izzy didn't stir.

She tiptoed past Mom and Dad's bedroom and into the kitchen. Raven opened the test tube and sniffed. It smelled like a mix of candy canes, hot cocoa, and pine trees. The label on the side said:

CANCELED SCHOOL WISH

Go outside. Remove the stopper.
Sprinkle three drops.
Stand back.

To return the wish to the tube, go to the wishing well,
and say three times, "I wish no more."

She couldn't go to school in the morning. This was her only hope. Raven unlocked the back door and stepped outside. The full moon shone on the garden, so she didn't need a flashlight to guide her to the middle of the yard.

Raven uncorked the bottle and slowly tipped it to the side. She held her breath and counted as the drops of white, shimmering liquid landed on the ground. "One, two..."

As the third drop hit the green grass, a white swirling mist drifted upward. It rose into the sky and erupted like a firework, showering Raven in gold sparks. And then...it simply vanished.

Raven waited, but nothing else happened. The wish had fizzled out. Whatever she was hoping would happen hadn't. Feeling silly, Raven went back inside. She would have to go to school after all.

CHAPTER 6

Wish Revealed

Early the next morning, Raven woke with a start. She'd been dreaming about everyone laughing at her. She was about to close her eyes again, but something was weird. Her bedroom was brighter than usual. Raven looked out her window and stared at the backyard. She couldn't believe it!

"What are you doing?" said Izzy, sitting up and rubbing her eyes. "Why are you at the window? Wait, is that...snow?" Izzy ran to the window and opened it. "Whoa! Snow! In May! In California?

This is amazing." She ran to her closet and pulled out sweaters and rain boots for them both. "Come on!"

Raven followed Izzy outside. They had to lift their knees to their chests to stomp through the deep snow. Izzy put her head back and stuck out her tongue to catch the falling flakes. "Let's make snow angels!" Izzy said, flopping backward. Raven copied her sister and fell into the snow. It felt like a wet, fluffy pillow. She didn't even mind as wetness crept down her neck. They swept their arms and legs to make perfect snow angels.

The sky turned orange as the sun rose, and the snow slowed to a few fat flakes here and there. Soon, all the kids from Lincoln Elementary would find out what had happened. Raven hugged herself. She had made it all happen. She started to tell Izzy, "Izzy, all this, it was…" but stopped in time. The Librarian's stern face in Raven's head reminded her of the rules. She couldn't tell anyone. No one would ever know Raven had made the winter wonderland.

"What were you going to say?" said Izzy.

"It doesn't matter."

Raven pulled Izzy to her feet and laughed. "Your eyelashes have turned frosty. Maybe we should go inside."

"No! How often do we get to play in snow?" pleaded Izzy. "Never—that's how often. A bit longer, please?"

Raven threw a snowball in answer. Izzy gasped but quickly made her own and threw it straight back. "Gotcha!"

Raven laughed and ducked out of the way as another snowball hurtled toward her. This time, Izzy's snowball sailed past Raven and hit their parents' bedroom window. *Splat!*

"What on earth?" Mom rubbed her eyes as she opened the bedroom window. She'd gotten home from her latest flight sometime in the night.

"Snow? Where did snow come from? It was supposed to be sunny today!" She noticed the girls. "What are you doing out there? It's freezing. Come inside, and I'll make some breakfast."

In the kitchen, puddles formed under Raven and Izzy as they thawed out with hot cocoa and chocolate chip pancakes. Raven breathed in the delicious chocolate smells. She was hungry after missing dinner the night before.

"I don't understand this weather!" said Mom. "I wonder what the weather report says."

Mom turned on the television. "A freak snowstorm hit the town of Lincoln today," the man on the screen said. "Meanwhile, the rest of the Bay Area is enjoying the hottest day of the year so far. We don't see any more snowstorms on the radar, so let's hope a thaw comes soon. In the meantime, enjoy the snow, and stay safe."

Raven looked at Mom. "Does this mean school is canceled?" She crossed her fingers for luck under the table.

"I wouldn't be surprised. No one will be able to get there in this." Mom's phone beeped with a message. She showed it to Raven: SNOW DAY DECLARED FOR LINCOLN ELEMENTARY.

"A snow day! I've never heard of that happening here in my whole life," said Mom.

Raven grinned. It had worked after all!

Just then the doorbell rang. "Who is that at this time of day?" said Mom.

"Mrs. Rose, could Raven come out to play in the snow?" Luca Flores stood at their door.

"Who are you?" Mom asked.

"My name is Luca. I just moved here," he said. "I sit next to Raven at school."

"In that case, of course!" Mom beckoned Raven to the door. "Off you go. Have fun! I'll make some more hot cocoa for when you kids are done. I won't be able to get to the airport today anyway."

Luca smiled at Raven and motioned her outside.

"Come on, let's take my sled to the top of the street and slide back down," said Luca, stomping through the snow and dragging his sled behind. "It's so much fun!"

"I didn't know you lived on our street," Raven said.

"You didn't ask," said Luca.

Raven blushed. He was right. She hadn't asked him anything. In fact, she'd ignored him, too wrapped up in her own problems.

"We only moved in last week, and most of our stuff is still in boxes. I can't believe I found my sled!"

"Where did you move from?"

"Breckenridge, Colorado. It's a ski town."

"I've never been skiing," Raven said.

"You'd love it. If it snows more, maybe we can find my skis!"

Raven hadn't thought of that. *How much snow were they going to get?*

CHAPTER 7

Zoo Trouble

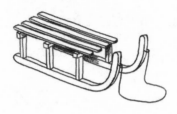

From the top of the street, kids whizzed down on sleds. The feeling in Raven's tummy was either fear or excitement. She'd never sledded before.

"Come on, Raven, you can go first." Luca patted the sled. Raven sat down, and Luca counted, "One, two, three." He gave a gentle shove, and Raven was off! Her hair swirled behind her as she laughed.

Luca shouted something. Over her shoulder, Raven saw him running down the hill, waving his arms. What was he yelling about? Before Raven had a chance to figure out...CRASH!

"Are you okay?" Luca asked when he caught up.

Raven sat up slowly. She'd broken the sled, crashing into Mr. Green's white picket fence. "I'm sorry about your sled! I'll get you a new one."

"It's not your fault. I forgot to tell you how to steer! Sorry about that," Luca said. "Let's go make a snowman. It's safer than sledding!"

This is loads more fun than sledding, thought Raven as they rolled giant balls of snow.

Together, they stacked the balls up and added sticks and stones for arms, eyes, and a mouth. For the finishing touches, Luca added his hat, and Raven put her gloves on the arms.

Raven hugged herself as they admired their creation. Her hands were cold, but her day off was all she could have wished for.

"I'm cold!" said Luca. "Do you think your mom would make us lunch?"

Raven's mom and dad were watching the news. A reporter was standing outside Lincoln Zoo.

"Lincoln is still struggling to cope as snow continues to fall. I'm at the town's zoo, where the snowstorm has left animals stranded. Keepers are unable to reach the enclosures due to snowdrifts. And those same snowdrifts could mean disaster for the zoo if any animals use them to climb out of their enclosures."

The cameras showed the gates blocked by snow. Raven couldn't believe it. The zoo was one

of her favorite places. Dad was a part-time keeper and often took them to visit. She loved watching the cute baby grizzly bear playing with its mama and chasing after its ball.

"Many of the zoo's animals are used to cold conditions. But without food, they could be in trouble soon. Back to the studio."

"Will the animals be okay?" asked Raven.

"I hope so," said Dad. "Maybe I can dig my way there to help out." He looked out the window and shook his head. "I hope this stops soon."

And for the first time since she'd made her wish, so did Raven.

That night, as Raven tried to fall asleep, all she could think about was the snow. She had gotten her wish. So the snow would surely stop overnight. Wouldn't it?

All night, Raven dreamed of giant snowmen, snowball battles, and never-ending snowstorms. In the morning, she opened the curtains, hoping to see that the snow had melted. Instead, the drifts in her yard stood even higher, and snow was falling again. From the TV downstairs, she could hear the news reporter: "Lincoln is still a winter wonderland today. Will it last until Memorial Day? It could be a cold start to summer for local residents!"

Mom sat at the kitchen table when Raven walked in. "Where's Izzy?" Raven asked.

"She's out back making a snowman."

"And Dad?"

"He's gone out to shovel the driveway so he can get to the zoo and I can get my car out. If I don't get to work today, I might not have a job to go back to."

"Mom, you can't drive in this!"

"I have to try, honey. I can't miss another flight."

The snow was fun at first. It meant no school and no presentation. But this wasn't fun anymore. Raven had to get to the Wish Library.

Dad walked in the front door and shook snow from his woolly hat. "Brrrrr. I need a warm drink now!"

"I'm so sorry about the animals," said Raven.

"Thank you." Dad rubbed her head. "But no need to apologize. You didn't make the snow, sweetie."

Raven wanted to cry. Everything had happened because of her. The snow, Luca's broken sled, Mom maybe losing her job, and the poor zoo animals starving. All because Raven had made a wish for school to be canceled. And she'd made the wish because she was too scared to present in front of her class.

Now, she had to fix it. She had to get back to the Wish Library and set everything back to normal. But with so much snow, would she be able to get to the schoolyard in time?

CHAPTER 8

A Plan

While Mom made breakfast, Raven quietly got dressed. She pulled on three sweaters, two pairs of leggings, gloves, a hat, a coat, and polka-dot rain boots. She checked the clock: 8:10.

Raven had three hours and one minute to return the wish. Normally, it took twenty minutes to walk to school, but this was no normal day. Plus, how would she find the wishing well entrance in the snow? Raven trembled at the thought. But she had no choice. If she didn't, the snow would stay forever. The zoo animals would starve. Her mom might lose her job. And Raven would be cursed with some unknown, terrible consequence.

Raven put the test tube in her backpack and crept out the front door. The snow had drifted across the street and made banks almost as high as her house. First, she needed to get to Luca's. He had something she needed.

Raven picked up Dad's shovel and started clearing a path. After five minutes, she pushed her glasses up her nose, wiped the sweat from her forehead, and looked back at the small distance she'd cleared. Shoveling was taking way too long.

Mom watched from the front door with her arms wrapped around herself. "Thank you for trying, my love," she said. "But it looks like we're stuck inside for another day! Come eat breakfast." Raven had no choice. She needed to regroup and rethink.

The microwave clock said 9:05. Raven had to find a way to leave the house again. Mom was on the phone to her manager explaining that she couldn't get to work. "I know it's sunny at the San Francisco airport, but down here, it's solid snow."

Just then, outside the kitchen where Raven was eating her oatmeal with maple syrup, a shovel broke through the wall of snow. Her neighbors had cleared a pathway! This was her chance.

Raven grabbed her backpack. She ran as fast as she dared on the slippery sidewalks. She almost fell *splat* on her butt a couple of times, but thanks to her soccer skills, she kept her balance.

At Luca's house, Raven hesitated. What if Luca wouldn't help her?

She had to try. Raven took a deep breath and rang the doorbell. She hoped he'd answer. Raven didn't want to talk to strangers, even if they were Luca's family.

Raven heard running footsteps, and the door opened. A girl who looked like a mini-Luca with pigtails stood in the warm doorway. "Hello, who are you?" she asked.

"Um. Hi. I'm Raven. Is Luca here?"

"LUCA!" she yelled. Then she said, "I like your glasses."

"Thanks," Raven replied.

"I'm Phoebe," said the girl.

Please let Luca appear soon, thought Raven. Time was running out.

"Phoebe! You're letting in all the cold air," said a woman's voice. "Oh! Hello. Don't stand there in the freezing cold. Come in!"

Raven went inside. "Is Luca here?"

"Oh, you must be Raven! I've heard so much about you!" said the woman. "I'm Luca's mom. Let me get you a warm drink. Luca's upstairs getting dressed."

Raven didn't have time. But she couldn't be rude.

"Raven!" Luca jumped down the stairs, two steps at a time. "Want to go sledding again? We can use Phoebe's sled."

"Raven is having a drink. Come sit, my love," said his mom. "I'm so happy Luca has made a friend. He's been so lonely since we moved here."

Raven had been missing Belle too much to think about that. Luca probably didn't know anyone here except her.

"Mom!" said Luca.

Luca's mom smiled. "I'll leave you two to it."

Once Luca's mom left the room, Raven blurted out, "Can I borrow your skis?"

He looked surprised. "Sure! Let's go skiing!"

"Um. Actually, I need to go on my own."

"Huh? Why?"

"I can't tell you."

"Is everything okay?"

"Yes. Well, no…It will be."

"Follow me," said Luca. "The skis are in the garage."

Raven was thankful he didn't ask any other questions. He seemed to trust her. Like a friend trusted another friend.

Raven waved goodbye to Phoebe, who was slurping hot cocoa.

"BYE, RAVEN!" she yelled.

"Shhhhhh!" Raven didn't want Luca's mom to see what they were doing. "Bye!" Raven whispered. Loud little sisters were something else she and Luca had in common.

In the garage, Luca showed her how to put on the boots and skis. He handed over some poles and helped her put her backpack on. "Are you sure about this?"

"Yes, I'm fine." She had to be fine. Telling anyone else about what she had to do would break the contract. Luca opened the garage door and pushed Raven out into the snow.

Now, she just had to get to school, find the well, stop the snow, and never ever, ever make another wish again.

CHAPTER 9

Animal Crossing

I can do this, Raven thought, shuffling the skis through the snow and using the poles to haul herself along. After five minutes, her arms ached, and she wanted to stop. But at least she was moving in the right direction.

Fifteen minutes later, she made it to the top of the hill that led to school. The way down was long, steep, and terrifying. Her heart felt like it would jump out of her chest. But she had no choice. Raven remembered the disaster with the sled. She hoped she wouldn't break Luca's skis too. Or a leg. She gave herself a countdown: "One, two, three...go!" Raven pushed with the poles, and off she flew!

A bump! Uh-oh. She soared into the air. Now she really was flying. The rushing air froze her face, and she clenched her hands around the ski poles. Raven screamed. This was it. She was going to crash again. She squeezed her eyes shut.

When Raven opened them, she was gliding. And she was still upright! She'd done it!

But when she looked ahead again, Raven let out another scream. In front of her, a parade of penguins was waddling across the street. With all the snow, they must have escaped from the zoo!

Raven weaved through the tall, awkward birds. Luckily, they were more interested in a row of trash cans that hadn't been collected than they were in her. Raven had to reverse the snowstorm before more animals escaped.

At the school gates, Raven unclipped the skis and inhaled the cold air. She'd made it. School was covered in a white comforter. It looked like no one had been there since the snowstorm.

Raven looked up at the tall fence. She was going to have to climb it.

"Grrrrrrrrrrrrr!"

Raven spun around. *What was that?* she wondered. *A dog? No, too loud.* She backed up against the fence. After a moment, the animal came out from its hiding place.

It's only the cute baby bear! Raven thought with relief.

But it looked hungry. And even as a baby, it was as almost as big as Raven. The bear cub stared at her. Raven had nowhere to go. She pushed herself flat against the fence, but her backpack was in the way.

Her backpack! Raven kept her eyes on the bear as it approached her. She shrugged her bag off her shoulders. With shaking hands, she unzipped it and grabbed her soccer ball. The bear gazed at the black-and-white ball Raven was holding.

"Fetch!" Raven shouted as she launched the ball away from the fence. Like a puppy, the grizzly bounded away through the snow.

Raven didn't wait to see what happened next. Without thinking, she grabbed on to the school fence and climbed. At the top, she paused to make sure the bear wasn't following her. It had found the ball and was playing, like in the zoo.

Now, she had to get to the Wish Library.

CHAPTER 10

I Wish No More!

Raven checked her watch: 10:41. Not long to get to the wishing well.

She tried to run to the trees at the end of the schoolyard. But the snow covered her knees, making it hard to even walk. It took forever to wade through it.

At last, she reached the giant chestnut trees, painted white by the snow. She walked in circles, searching for the stone well. Her foot hit something hard. Raven bent down and dug through the snow. She wished she'd brought Dad's shovel! At last, she uncovered a...big rock. No! Where was the well?

Raven had an idea. She took the test tube from her pocket, held it out, and chanted, "I wish no more. I wish no more. I wish no more." Maybe if she was near the well, it would reverse the wish, even if she couldn't see the Wish Library entrance itself.

Raven kept trying. "I wish no more. I wish no more. I wish no more." It wasn't working. *Maybe I'm in the wrong place*, thought Raven.

Then, a few feet away, something glittering caught her eye. A gold coin! She trudged over to pick it up and tripped. "Ouch!" Could it be the well this time? Raven dug through the icy snow. Yes! She saw the circle of stones and the old bucket. Just in time too. It was 11:08.

"I wish no more. I wish no more. I wish no more," said Raven.

As she did, a loud, swirling snow tornado

erupted around her. Raven fell to the ground and covered her head with one hand and held the test tube out with the other. She squeezed her eyes shut. The test tube vibrated and got hot, but she kept hold of it. She couldn't lose it. Not when she was so close to returning the wish and ending the snow nightmare.

Suddenly, it was silent. Raven opened her eyes and looked up. The snow had vanished. Lincoln Elementary was gray and brown as usual. The schoolyard was green again. And the trees around her even had purple blossoms. It was like the wish had never happened.

A flashing neon sign with a down arrow appeared above the well: RETURN CHUTE.

Raven dropped in the test tube and watched it fall. Suddenly, she was tumbling through the darkness too. She wasn't as scared this time because she knew how it would end. Sure enough, she landed on the trampoline at the feet of the Librarian.

"We have a return! Would you like to renew your wish?"

"No. Way," Raven said.

"As you wish. Or as you don't wish." The Librarian chuckled at her own joke. She pushed

some buttons on her computer and waited. "Excellent, all drops of the wish are present and correct. No fines for you!"

Raven breathed a deep sigh of relief.

"Do you want to try a new wish?" The Librarian peered at her. "A baby brother perhaps? Or the ability to fly?"

Wishes are more trouble than they are worth, thought Raven.

"I don't wish for anything," she said. The Librarian didn't seem to hear as she stared at her computer. "Other than to go home."

"You know the way," said the Librarian without looking.

Raven was almost at the door when the Librarian spoke again. "Excellent!" she said. "We have a new customer." The computer whirred, and a piece of paper printed. "Oh, this is interesting!"

Before Raven could ask what exactly was so interesting, a person bounced off the trampoline and landed on the ground with a thud.

"Welcome to the Wish Library!" the Librarian boomed.

The person was bundled in winter clothes. But when they stood up, Raven recognized the face right away. "Luca!"

Luca rubbed his head. His eyes grew wide as he took in the Wish Library. "Raven? What is this place?"

CHAPTER 11

A Second Wish

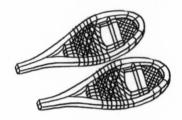

"How did you get here?" Raven asked.

"I followed you," said Luca. "You were being so strange, and I was worried." He waggled his feet. He was wearing what looked like tennis rackets on his feet. "I saw you throw the ball at the bear! That was so cool!"

Something fluttered in Raven's stomach. Luca had been there to help the whole time, just like Belle would have been.

"When I reached the trees at the end of the

field, everything went white," Luca continued. "And then the snow vanished! I found a gold coin and a well. And everyone knows what you do with a coin and a well."

Raven took a deep breath. After everything they had been through, she owed Luca an explanation. She told him about Belle leaving and their project together and her wish to cancel school. "It all turned out wrong," Raven said at last. "All because I was scared."

"You don't seem scared to me," said Luca.

"I am. If I present to everyone, I'll go bright red and cry. Everyone will think I'm a baby."

"If you were scared, you wouldn't have gotten back here. You had to ski past those penguins! And get past a grizzly bear! All in a snowstorm."

Raven shook her head. "Those things were easy compared to public speaking. Besides, I'm good at sports."

"Well, you explained all of this pretty well," said Luca, waving his arms around the Wish Library.

"Even if I still don't know how this place exists."

Raven thought of something. There was only one way for Luca to get into the Wish Library. "What did you wish for?" Raven asked. "The entrance only reveals itself to someone who truly needs to make a wish."

"I can answer that," said the Librarian, waving the slip of paper. "According to the computer, your young friend here wished for..." The Librarian said the word *friend* with a slight smile.

"Wait!" said Luca, turning red. "It's okay. You don't need to say it."

"As you wish," replied the Librarian.

"We should get home." Raven led the way to the exit.

"Hold on," said Luca. "I want to explore. What's that?" Luca pointed at the giant computer. "And what are all these?" He waved at the racks of rainbow test tubes.

"Over here we have—" the Librarian said.

"Nope!" Raven interrupted. "Come on, Luca. We need to get home."

"As you wish," said the Librarian. "See you next time."

"Not likely," Raven muttered.

"I don't know. It could be fun to try out a wish sometime," said Luca. "Flying sounds fun."

"No way!" said Raven. "Wishes are too much trouble."

CHAPTER 12

Upside-Down Friends

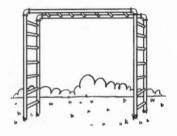

"Happy Monday!" said Ms. Earl, clapping her hands in delight. "I'm so happy we're back at school after our funny weather last week."

Funny weather was a mild way to describe the snowstorm Raven had caused. At least no one knew it was her. Well, apart from Luca. On the way home from the Wish Library, he plotted what wish to make next, even though Raven reminded him what a terrible wish she'd made. "Yes! But now we know what can go wrong. So we will make a better choice."

They'd walked by the zoo on the way to school. The penguins and grizzly bear were back in their enclosures, and the keepers were feeding the other animals. Raven's mom was back to work on another trip. Raven was relieved everything was back to normal. She was even relieved to be back at school. Even if it meant...

"I was so sad we missed out on Voices of History day, but as I said in my email over the weekend, I've rearranged our schedule so we can do it today! Raven Rose, come to the board, please, to present your project."

Raven pushed her curls off her face and nudged her glasses up her nose. They slid straight back down. She stood and straightened the coat Dad had found in a vintage store. She put on a matching hat and carried a large brown handbag. In her other hand, she clutched her poster.

Raven walked to Ms. Earl at the board and took the wooden pointer with the owl on the end. In large letters across the top of the poster, she'd

written, "THREE THINGS ABOUT NELLIE BLY." She pointed at her portrait of a woman dressed like Raven. "This is me, Nellie Bly."

Raven paused. She felt a bit wobbly, but she remembered how she'd felt when she'd skied down the hill. Luca gave her a thumbs-up. She kept talking, her voice getting stronger as she felt braver. "In 1889, I took a challenge. I said I could travel all the way around the world in fewer than eighty days."

Everyone in the class was smiling, their eyes fixed on Raven. "I was a journalist, so I wrote about my journey, and it was published in the *New York Post*." Raven turned to point at the pictures on the poster. "I traveled by boat, train, and even horse. I arrived back in New York seventy-two days after I left."

Finally, Raven turned back to face the classroom. "Nellie Bly was a brave and adventurous woman. She inspired other women to do brave things too. And girls like me."

Raven took a quick bow, and everyone in the room clapped. Luca clapped the loudest.

"Thank you for sharing, Raven. It was worth the wait," said Ms. Earl. "Okay Room Twenty-Three, let's tidy our desks and get ready for recess. After, we'll hear some more presentations."

Raven smiled. It hadn't been as bad as she had expected. She felt brave like Nellie Bly. And brave like Raven Rose. The girl who'd faced a bear and saved Lincoln from a snowstorm. Yes, a snowstorm she'd caused. But also the snowstorm she'd stopped.

As usual, during recess, Raven hung upside down on the monkey bars. But today, someone hung next to her.

"This is kind of fun!" Luca said.

"You never told me what you wished for," Raven said.

Luca's cheeks turned red. "For a friend," he replied. "But I didn't need to make a wish after all." They both smiled.

"I have an idea. After school, let's go get..." Raven started.

"Frozen yogurt!" finished Luca. "I wish I had a bottomless bowl of chocolate hazelnut frozen yogurt with sprinkles and mini-marshmallows."

Raven turned to her friend. Her upside-down and right-side-up friend.

"Be careful what you wish for!"